I Was a Mouseketeer!

Kieran Scott

Disney PRESS

New York

For Erin . . . for obvious reasons

Printed in the United States of America

First Edition

Book Design by Charles Kreloff

1 3 5 7 9 10 8 6 4 2

Library of Congress Catalog Card Number: 2001088826

ISBN 0-7868-4470-1

For more Disney Press fun, visit www.disneybooks.com

Table of Contents

 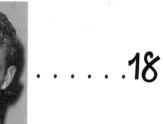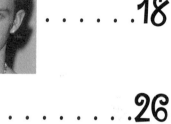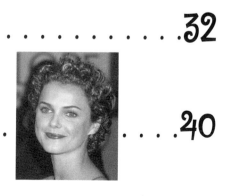

The "New" Mickey

What do Britney Spears, Christina Aguilera, Justin Timberlake, JC Chasez, and Keri Russell all have in common? Aside from the fact that they're supertalented, all five of these stars grew up on Disney Channel as Mouseketeers!

When *The Mickey Mouse Club* burst onto Disney Channel in April 1989, there was music, there was laughter, there was dancing . . . and there were a lot of people who thought it was a bad idea. Sure the club was a huge hit in the '50s, but were mouse ears, kooky skits, and wholesome teens going to play in the almost '90s?

"We had a lot of skepticism about doing *The Mickey Mouse Club* in the 1990s," Steve Fields, then senior vice president of Disney Channel, told the *San Jose Mercury News* in 1989. "But so many elements [of the old show] were terrific, and kids still relate to kids."

Even the most famous 1950s Mouseketeer, Annette Funicello, had her doubts. But once she viewed an advance tape of the show, she did a total 180. "After seeing it, I realized that kids will want to tune in just like they did with us," Annette told *TV Guide* in 1990.

And she couldn't have been more right. *The Mickey Mouse Club* was a huge hit with teens and 'tweens, and before anyone could blink, the Mouseketeers were being featured in entertainment magazines across the country and screaming fans were lining up at Disney/MGM Studios for a chance to see a taping of the show.

While the producers made the wise decision of ditching the mouse ears, the show stayed true to the original program's format. Each day had a theme. Monday was Music Day, featuring top musical artists like New Kids on the Block or Michael Damian. Tuesday was Guest Day, when a lucky *MMC* viewer got the chance to spend

Mouse Club

a day with the celebrity of his or her choice. Wednesday was Anything Can Happen Day, which included silly themes, wacky stunts, surprise guest appearances, and games. Thursday was Party Day, when the cast would come together for a theme party, which always included a skit and a dance number. Finally, Friday was Hall of Fame Day, when the show would honor kids who had done great things and present them with the Mickey Award.

But there was a lot more going on than just the theme days. The cast members appeared in music videos, acted in comedic skits, got down in some innovative dance numbers, played games with audience members, and kept up a crazy level of energy the entire time. And it couldn't have been easy. On top of recording songs, learning dance numbers, rehearsing, and taping a show that aired five days a week, these kids still had to go to school!

Hall of Fame Day participants

Mouse Club Facts

The original *Mickey Mouse Club* debuted on ABC on October 3, 1955.

The original cast consisted of twenty-four kids and two adult cohosts.

Three additional boys were originally cast, but they were fired for "rambunctious and disrespectful behavior" before the first show was taped.

The show ran in the United States from 1955 to 1959, with a total of thirty-nine Mouseketeers.

The program was an hour long and cartoons were a huge portion of the show.

The Mickey Mouse Club was eventually dubbed in Spanish, French, German, Italian, and Japanese.

The original Mouseketeers were educated in two cherry-red trailers they called their "little red schoolhouses."

Aside from the mouse ears, the Mouseketeers' uniforms consisted of blue pleated skirts or pants, off-white short-sleeved turtleneck sweaters with their names in black block letters across the front and the *Mickey Mouse Club* logo on the back, and black tap shoes. (You can bet the new Mouseketeers were glad to wear their varsity jackets instead!)

Disney Channel's *MMC* celebrates its 100th episode!

Cast members throughout the seven-season run of *The Mickey Mouse Club* ranged in age from eleven to seventeen. So how did they fit school into their hectic schedule? Here's what a normal day was like for a Mouseketeer:

7:00 A.M.
Rise and shine! Everyone grabs a breakfast that will help them keep going for a seriously long day.

8:30 A.M.
The bus arrives. (Cast members, along with at least one parent, lived right near the Disney/MGM Studios soundstage.)

9:00 A.M.—12:30 P.M.
Cast members attend school with special tutors.

12:30 P.M.—1:00 P.M.
Lunch at the cafeteria-like commissary at Disney/MGM Studios.

1:00 P.M.—4:00 P.M.
Rehearse, rehearse, rehearse!

4:00 P.M.—7:00 P.M.
Tape the show in front of a live studio audience.

7:00 P.M.— Whenever
Dinner, homework, and early to bed to get ready for another crazy day.

Of course, it wasn't all work and no play. On breaks, the Mouseketeers would play basketball, Rollerblade, or even hit a few rides at the Magic Kingdom right next door. Plus, they got to meet famous and inspiring people, and do what they loved—perform.

Seasons One and Two

April–June 1989 and October–December 1989

When the show debuted in 1989, there were twelve Mouseketeers: Albert, Tiffini, Chase, Jennifer, Damon, Deedee, David, Brandy, Braden, Lindsey, Josh, and Roque, and two adult co-hosts: Fred Newman and Mowava Pryor. Each week the Club would premiere one Video Jam—a music video recorded and mixed outside the studio. The other skits, games, and dance numbers would be performed on, in, and around a rotating diner set in the middle of the soundstage, or on a city-street set that ran along the side of the stage. There were also Mickey Mouse Club movies. The Club would show a few minutes of the movie three times a week, until the film was complete. (If you thought your favorite stars were the only ones to jump-start their careers on the Club, check out our sidebar for a peek at some of the well-known actors who appeared in MMC movies!)

In the second season, David and Braden left the show, and Kevin joined the cast, but the format basically remained the same.

Season Three

October–December 1990

After almost a year of reruns, *MMC* returned with new episodes and new members. Roque was gone, but there were five new kids on the scene—Marc, Mylin, Ilana, Jason, and Ricky. The Club got an infusion of younger talent with these new Mouseketeers and the dance numbers became bigger and more complicated.

Season Four

September–October 1991

The fourth season of *MMC* brought the biggest changes yet. Brandy left the Club to pursue an acting career, and five of the

Where it all began for . . .

Jason Priestley—The 90210 hottie starred as Buzz, a rebel-turned-angel, in two MMC films, *Teen Angel* and *Teen Angel Returns.*

Jennie Garth—Jennie and Jason first worked together on *Teen Angel Returns* before hitting Beverly Hills. Jennie also appeared in the MMC film, *Just Perfect.*

Kelli Williams—Kelli was a girl-next-door in *My Life as a Babysitter,* and now plays a lawyer on *The Practice.*

Brian Krause—*Charmed's* guardian angel once played a tennis-lovin' cutie in *Match Point.*

Christopher Daniel Barnes—You know him now as Greg in the Brady Bunch films. We knew him then as a boy with a mischievous dog in *Just Perfect.*

Shannen Doherty—Another 90210 star! Shannen appeared in *The Secret of Lost Creek* before making her way to a more upscale zip code, and then on to sorcery in *Charmed.*

Amanda Foreman—Amanda appeared in the MMC movie *My Life as a Babysitter.* Now she plays Meghan Rotundi, the girl you love to hate on *Felicity.*

other original members—Chase, Deedee, Damon, Albert, and Tiffini—formed the pop group The Party. They were now spending most of their time in the recording studio, touring, and making TV appearances, but they still stopped by the Club once in a while to perform some of their original songs and hang with the cast. Adult co-host Mowava Pryor also left the show, and was replaced by Terri Misner.

Another big change that year was a huge group of fresh faces. Joining the Club were Keri, JC, Tony, Tasha, Terra, Rhona, Matt, Dale, Nita, and Blain. It was the biggest cast shift since the show began, and there was definitely a new energy in the air. The show had celebrated its one hundredth episode the season before, and was enjoying the height of its popularity. The soundstage was opened up to provide for bigger, more production-heavy musical numbers. In the beginning, the Club would stage abbreviated versions of contemporary hits and classic tunes. Now the diner set could be removed, and the Mouseketeers could perform entire songs, making music a more integral element of the show.

Club movie, *Emerald Cove*. The whole cast got to participate in this *Dawson's Creek* meets *California Dreaming* sudser. With a band, a few love triangles, and some serious comedy, *Emerald Cove* would become a Mouse Club staple until the show wrapped.

Season Six

October–December 1993

In the sixth season, the Club lost a bunch of members (Mylin, Terra, Jason, Kevin, Tasha, and Blain), but got another group of young Mouseketeers to liven things up. Britney, Christina, Justin, Ryan, Nikki, T.J., and Tate joined the Club and showed everyone that young kids can have big voices too.

The Club recorded thirty-six episodes that season, which were shown on Monday through Thursday, with a rerun from the week airing on Friday.

Season Seven

May 1995–February 1996

In the seventh and final season, Tiffini and Chase came back to the Club and Keri left to pursue acting full-time. Disney Channel started airing episodes only once a week, on Thursday, with the episode repeating on Sunday. They stretched the final forty-four episodes over ten months and then bid farewell to one of the most successful teen variety shows ever made.

With more than three hundred episodes aired in less than seven years, there was no disputing the fact that the Mouseketeers had done their fair share of entertaining—but many of them had only just begun.

Season Five

October–November 1992 and June–July 1993

The same group of performers ushered the show into its fifth season, when the Club took a new tack with the Mouse Club movie. The first movie exclusively starring Mouseketeers was called *The Prescott Press* and was about a group of teens who wanted to put out a quality high school newspaper. Eight members of the Club acted in the movie, including Keri Russell. That season also saw the debut of another Mouse

Bri

tney Spears

T he way Britney and her family and friends tell the story, she always seemed destined to be a Mouseketeer. Britney was dancing from the moment she could walk and singing from the moment she could talk. She was constantly performing for her family—so constantly that they'd sometimes beg her to keep it down. But all Britney wanted to do was perform, and there was no stopping her.

Britney grew up in the small town of Kentwood, Louisiana. Like a lot of little girls, she took tap and ballet lessons from a very early age. *Unlike* a lot of little girls, she won first place at a local talent competition at the age of five, and the title of Miss Talent USA at the age of seven. Dancing and singing weren't her only skills—Britney was also fabulous at gymnastics and won a bunch of state titles at her level. But at the age of eight, Britney decided to give up the three hours of gymnastics practice a day and focus on dance.

1st Grade; Park Lane Academy, McComb, MS

She joined a dance troupe and traveled through Louisiana. It was during this time that Britney first heard about the auditions for *The*

"God gave me a talent to perform and I know I have it in me. I can't just coop it up."

—*Britney Spears Stylin!*

Full name: Britney Jean Spears

Nicknames: Brit, Bit-Bit

Birthday: December 2, 1981

Sign: Sagittarius

Birthplace: Kentwood, Louisiana

Height: 5´4˝

Hair: light brown

Eyes: brown

Parents: mother, Lynne Spears; father, Jamie Spears

Siblings: sister, Jamie Lynn; brother, Bryan

Favorite color: baby blue

Favorite food: her mom's chicken dumplings

Favorite music: pop

Favorite performers: Mariah Carey, Whitney Houston, Madonna, Goo Goo Dolls, Third Eye Blind

Favorite TV shows: *Friends* and *Felicity*

Favorite movies: *My Best Friend's Wedding*, *Steel Magnolias*

Favorite actors: Tom Cruise, Ben Affleck, Meg Ryan

Favorite sports teams: the Chicago Bulls and the New York Yankees

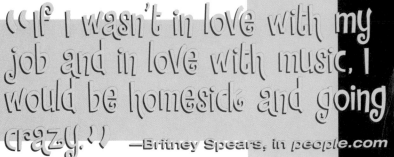

Mickey Mouse Club that were being held in cities across the country. The closest audition site was in Atlanta, Georgia, so Britney and her mom hopped in the car and made the almost five hundred-mile trek so that Britney could strut her stuff. She was up against hundreds of kids (and that was just the Atlanta auditions), all competing for ten to twelve open spots on the show.

Britney gave it everything she had and thought she'd nailed the audition. She was, in fact, one of seven finalists in Atlanta, but then came the devastating news—she was just too young for the Club. Britney was crushed! She'd always been a huge Disney fan and this seemed like the perfect gig. But the trip to Atlanta wasn't a waste. One of the casting directors told Britney's mom that her daughter had some major talent and recommended an agent in New York. It was a big change from Kentwood, but Britney and her mother headed for the Big Apple.

Once they were there, Britney took classes at the Broadway Dance Studio and the Professional Performing Arts School. She landed parts in national commercials for products like Mitsubishi and Days

Britney and Justin love being the center of attention!

Inn. Then, in 1991, Britney snagged a part in an off-Broadway show called *Ruthless!* At first, Britney was an understudy in the musical comedy, but when the lead child left the show, Britney won the role.

In 1992, Britney left New York and went back home to attend school. She thought she just wanted a normal life, but it wasn't long before she started missing showbiz. That summer Britney heard about an open call for the show *Star Search*—a television talent competition—in Baton Rouge, LA, and she knew she had to go.

Britney blew the *Star Search* people away and they told her they wanted her for the show, which taped in Los Angeles. Suddenly Britney and her mom were jetting to the other coast. Britney was nervous about performing on national television, but she didn't have to be. She sang her heart out and won her first round, beating out the little girl who had been the champion the week before. Britney got to return the following week, but this time, she lost to a boy.

At this point, Britney could have been discouraged and hung up her microphone for good, but it just so happened that it was audition time again back at *The Mickey Mouse Club*. Britney was now eleven years old—still younger than any Mouseketeer that had appeared on the Club—but she didn't let that stop her. This time, she was up against over 15,000 kids and had to go through a three-day-long screen test. It was grueling, but Britney was one of seven kids chosen as new members of the Club.

"It was like a dream come true," Britney

"The thing that I always remember about her is that she just had that glow about her. When I saw her dance, I knew she was going to be something more than just a cast member on a TV show."

—Justin Timberlake on Britney's *MMC* years, in *CosmoGIRL! Online*

"There are Britney people and non-Britney people."

—Britney Spears, in *ELLE*

said in *Pop People: Britney!*. "It was all I'd really wanted since I was eight. They called on the phone and said, 'You're going to be a Mouseketeer,' and I just started screaming."

Britney, her mother, and her little sister Jamie Lynn all moved to Orlando so Britney could take the stage as the youngest member ever of *The Mickey Mouse Club*. At first, she performed as a backup singer and dancer, but she was quickly featured in a duet with her new friend Justin Timberlake on the song "I Feel for You," and sang solo in "I'm Gonna Get You." Britney got to display her amazing dance moves and her larger-than-life voice. People were stunned by her talent.

Britney also got to show off her acting skills, taking part in comedic skits about everything from strict parents to Elvis to really big shoes. She loved performing, but has said her favorite part of being on the Club was being with the other Mouseketeers. Not only did she form lasting friendships with fellow cast members like Justin, Christina, JC, and Ryan, but she had older kids around to look up to.

"I used to really idolize Keri Russell," Britney wrote in *Britney Spears' Heart to Heart.* "She was older and a great dancer, and I wished I had her beautiful long curly hair."

While Britney was having a good time with all her new friends, she was also learning what it was really like to be a professional performer. The schedule was hectic, but it was all worth it. Why? Because if it wasn't for the Club, Britney may never have become the star she is today.

"When Britney's album was about to come out, I thought about calling radio stations to request her song. Then she blew up and I was like, 'She doesn't need me!'"

—Christina Aguilera, in *YM*

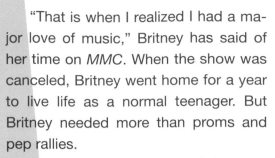

"That is when I realized I had a major love of music," Britney has said of her time on *MMC*. When the show was canceled, Britney went home for a year to live life as a normal teenager. But Britney needed more than proms and pep rallies.

"Going into the middle of the year, she was antsy," Britney's mother told *people.com*. Britney missed singing, dancing, and working her tail off. She made a demo tape and her mom sent it to an entertainment lawyer in New York named Larry Rudolph. He signed on as her co-manager and eventually helped Britney land a deal at Jive Records.

The rest is history. Britney's first album and single, both titled *. . . Baby One More Time*, went to number one simultaneously, making her the youngest performer ever to have both an album and a single at number one at the same time. She toured with her friends, the members of 'NSYNC, in the summer of 1998, gathering a huge fan base. For the next few years, Britney never stopped—making appearances on MTV, guest-starring on *Sabrina the Teenage Witch* and *The Simpsons,* among other shows, making videos, and recording her second album. *Oops! I Did it Again* broke even more records—selling more albums in one week than any other album by a solo female performer. Britney headlined her own tour this time, bringing down the house in venues across the country.

"I remember I read this harsh review about my show, and one of my friends told me that this was the exact same stuff people said about Madonna. And it's like, she didn't care. Madonna just came out and was herself," Britney told *ELLE*. "I respect that a lot."

These days, Britney's earning a lot of respect herself.

"Even before [Britney's] next video comes out, people are demanding to see it."

—Tom Calderone, Senior VP of music and talent for MTV, in *ELLE*

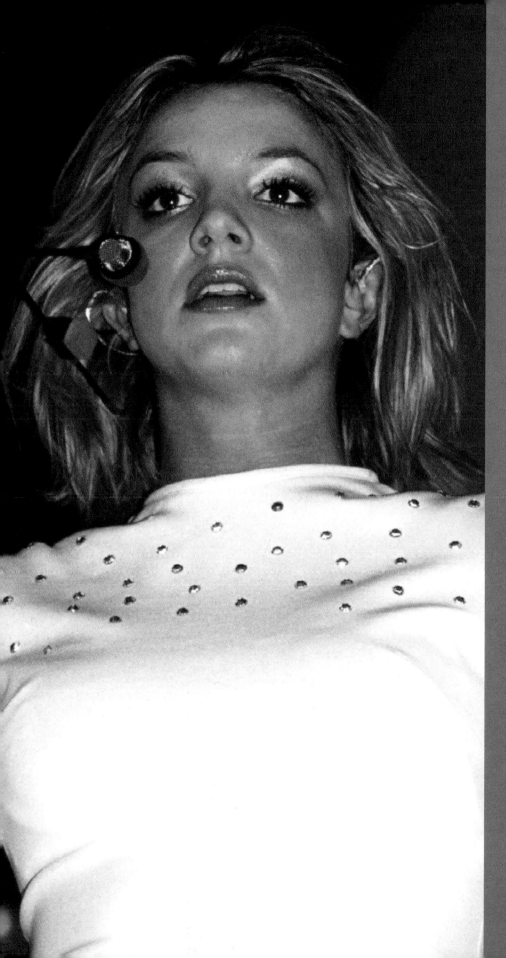

Britney Facts

Britney first met Justin Timberlake and pop star Jessica Simpson at her *MMC* audition in 1992. Unfortunately, Jessica didn't make the final cut.

Britney wants to go to college and study entertainment law.

Britney's favorite rides at Walt Disney World are Space Mountain and the Rock 'N Roller Coaster.

At the age of five, Britney sang "What Child Is This?" at her kindergarten graduation.

Britney has a Yorkie named Bitsy who accompanies her on tour.

The concept for Britney's first video, . . . *Baby One More Time*, was all Britney. She wanted something teens could relate to, and she wanted to show off her moves. (Originally, the video was supposed to be a cartoon.)

When Britney first started touring with 'NSYNC, the crowd wasn't too psyched to see her. It was mostly girls who wanted to see the guys they loved, and they had no idea who Britney was.

justin

Timberlake

I n the summer of 2000, when Britney and Justin finally told the world they were boyfriend and girlfriend, no one was surprised—there had been rumors about their relationship forever. But it's even less surprising when you find out how similar their paths to fame were.

Like Britney, Justin grew up in a small southern town. He came from a house full of music. His uncle, grandmother, and father were all great singers and Justin credits them with his talent and love of song. "I pretty much popped out singing," Justin said in 'NSYNC: The Official Book. His father sang in a bluegrass band and the family would often travel to see him perform. When Justin was just three, he taught

8th Grade; E.E. Jeter Elementary School, Millington, TN

Full name: Justin Randall Timberlake

Nicknames: Shot, Curly, Mr. Smooth

Birthday: January 31, 1981

Sign: Aquarius

Birthplace: Memphis, Tennessee

Height: 6´

Hair: light brown

Eyes: blue

Parents: mother, Lynn Harless; father, Randy Timberlake; stepfather, Paul Harless; stepmother, Lisa Timberlake

Siblings: half-brothers Jonathan and Steven

Favorite color: baby blue

Favorite foods: cereal and pasta

Favorite music: hip-hop, R&B

Favorite performers: Brian McKnight, Take 6

Favorite TV shows: The Simpsons and South Park

Favorite movie: The Usual Suspects

Favorite actors: Brad Pitt, Samuel L. Jackson, Halle Berry, Sandra Bullock

Favorite sports team: the Orlando Magic

"I'm just a very passionate person in everything I do. I really believe that whenever you do something you should put everything into it; otherwise, it's really not worth it."

—Justin Timberlake, in CosmoGIRL!

himself to harmonize to music—a skill it takes some people a lifetime to learn.

As a child, Justin sang in the choir at his Baptist church and played a lot of basketball. He says he was always performing and messing around, but he also had a serious side. His mother has said that Justin was a very private kid and valued time alone. He'd often play in his room by himself, and he did very well in school. He got his first B in third grade and was devastated. Justin's mother helped him learn that no one can be perfect all the time. Still, just as he did when he was little, Justin strives to be the best he can be at everything he does.

When Justin was in fourth grade, his love of music got him his first little break. He and a bunch of his friends put together a New Kids on the Block lip-synching act for a school talent show. But instead of lip-synching the whole thing, Justin actually sang a song originally sung by Joey McIntyre—"Please Don't Go Girl." He was a huge hit and the boys were asked to perform again at a neighboring school. They went all out, even dressing up as the different members of NKOTB. At this performance, the girls in the audience went crazy and ended up chasing Justin and his friends down the hallway as if they were the actual New Kids.

"Little girls in sixth, seventh, eighth, and ninth grades just surrounded him," Justin's stepfather told *people.com*. "They had him pinned up against a wall. Some wanted to get his autograph."

After that, Justin's mom knew her kid had some serious star potential. Justin got a vocal coach and started entering some amateur contests in and around Memphis and even performed at the Grand Ole Opry. Then, less than a year after his grade-school stage debut, *Star Search* held a talent search at a mall in Memphis and Justin saw his opportunity. He went to the casting call and the producers were floored by this little boy's huge talent. They chose him to appear on the show. Justin couldn't believe it!

The show was taped in Orlando, so Justin and his mom hopped a plane with high hopes. Justin, wearing a cowboy hat, performed a country tune called "Sounds Like Love's Got a Hold on You." Unfortunately, he did not win his first round. But there was an up-side to the whole experience. His episode was taped on the soundstage right next to the set of *The Mickey Mouse Club*. Justin watched *MMC* all the time and was a huge fan, so when he found out the club would be holding an open casting call in Nashville, he was there.

Justin auditioned with thousands of kids and was chosen as a finalist. Then he headed to an *MMC* casting camp with other finalists—including Britney—and they both made the final cut. Justin was one of seven kids chosen out of tens of thousands from across the country. This was the big time, and Justin couldn't wait to get to Orlando. Once he was there, he wasted no time making friends on the set.

First there was Britney. The two hit it off right away and were constantly paired up for duets on the show. Britney told *TV Guide* that she and Justin were always together and even ate their lunches alone together in their dressing rooms sometimes, just to get away from

The whole gang is here.

the craziness. "We had a lot of things in common because we were both raised in the same kind of southern family that taught us to have manners, honesty, loyalty, and honor . . . we had a lot of the same culture and upbringing," Justin told *CosmoGIRL! online*.

But Brit wasn't his only pal on the set. Justin once told reporters he and Ryan Gosling were "partners in crime," and he also became fast friends with JC Chasez. "JC was the cool, older guy, and Justin wanted to be just like him," Christina Aguilera told *Rolling Stone*.

After *MMC* wrapped, Justin went home to Tennessee for a year, but didn't take well to being back in Normalsville. "I really started to find myself there [on the Club]. It was a good experience. After that, I went back to school for a year and got into trouble—mailbox bashing and just being a delinquent," Justin told *Rolling Stone*. Sounds like Justin was itching to perform again—just like Britney. Luckily, he wouldn't have to wait long.

JC stopped in Memphis to visit Justin on his way back from Los Angeles, where he'd gone after the Club was canceled. Together, the two friends started writing songs and recording demos—giving Justin a more positive outlet for his wealth of energy. At the same time, Chris Kirkpatrick, whom Justin had met while in Orlando, called Justin to find out if he'd be interested in getting a group together. Psyched at the prospect of performing again, JC and Justin met up with Chris in Orlando. They asked their friend, Joey Fatone, who was then performing at the theme parks, to join up with them, but still needed a bass singer. At first, they hooked up with a guy named Jason, but when he didn't work out, Justin's vocal coach recommended Lance Bass. Lance flew in from Mississippi, and everyone just clicked. 'NSYNC was formed.

Now, six years later, what these guys have done together is legendary. They first toured

Justin says the guys in 'NSYNC are really the only people he trusts to be honest with him because they're all in the same position.

Germany and became huge stars in Europe, but U.S. fame wasn't far behind. Their debut album, 'NSYNC, went diamond—selling more than ten million copies! Their third album, *No Strings Attached*, broke all one-week sales records with 2.4 million copies sold, their tour sold out venues across the country, and the album spawned the band's first number one hit, "It's Gonna Be Me."

Now, the band has struck a deal to make a film together, and Justin has already made his post-Club acting debut in the TV movie *Model Behavior*. But his first priority outside the band isn't acting, it's his charity organization, the Justin Timberlake Foundation, which raises money to improve music education in schools. This is an important cause for Justin because he says the program at his school was awful and if his mom hadn't taken him to voice lessons outside school, he wouldn't be where he is today.

"Music is another way for young minds and young bodies to get all those negative energies out," Justin told *Rolling Stone*.

In a time when a lot of pop stars want to project a cool, dangerous image and cause controversy, Justin isn't afraid to be a positive role model and promote education.

If the guys in 'NSYNC have a costume where they each have to wear the same piece in a different color, Justin always gets first dibs on anything baby blue. It's "his" color and the rest of the guys know it.

Justin Facts

Justin's mom manages the all-girl group, Innosense. (Former Mouseketeer Nikki DeLoach is a member.)

In grade school Justin hated his hair because kids used to call him Brillo Pad. He even tried to cut it all off once, earning himself his one and only spanking.

Growing up, Justin's heroes were Michael Jackson and Michael Jordan.

Justin's first car was a Mercedes jeep. His second was a BMW convertible.

Justin's lucky number is twenty-one because it was his jersey number In basketball, and one of his earliest nicknames was Bounce because of his abilities on the court.

Justin collects sneakers. At last count he had more than seventy pairs.

When Justin sang "This I Promise You" at the live concert from Madison Square Garden, he was singing right to Britney, who was sitting in front of him in the audience.

Someone once asked Justin for his autograph, thinking he was actor Ryan Phillippe.

JC Chasez

When journalists write about Joshua "JC" Chasez, the same few words always seem to come up—"intense," "focused," "serious," and "energetic." Justin refers to JC as "the serious music guy" and JC himself says that no matter what he does, he throws himself into it one hundred percent.

As a child growing up in the small town of Bowie, Maryland, JC was adventurous and athletic, but he also spent a lot of time by himself. He learned to play the piano and often played at family gatherings, accompanying the family when they sang Christmas carols together. Even though JC didn't mind using his great singing voice in front of his family, getting him to sing in public was a whole other story.

While JC's mom says he was painfully shy, JC attributes his unwillingness to get

Freshman year; Bowie High School, Bowie, MD

> "They want to have a good time, and when they go to the show, we just want to entertain the heck out of them."
>
> —JC on 'NSYNC's fans, in *Rolling Stone*

Full name: Joshua Scott Chasez

Nicknames: Mr. Serious, Big Daddy, Shazaam, Sleepy

Birthday: August 8, 1976

Sign: Leo

Birthplace: Washington, D.C.

Height: 5'11"

Hair: brown

Eyes: blue

Parents: mother, Karen Chasez; father, Roy Chasez

Siblings: sister, Heather; brother, Tyler

Favorite color: blue

Favorite foods: Chinese, mint chocolate-chip ice cream

Favorite music: pop

Favorite performers: Sting, Seal

Favorite TV show: *Friends*

Favorite movies: The *Star Wars* trilogy and the *Indiana Jones* trilogy

Favorite sports team: the Washington Redskins

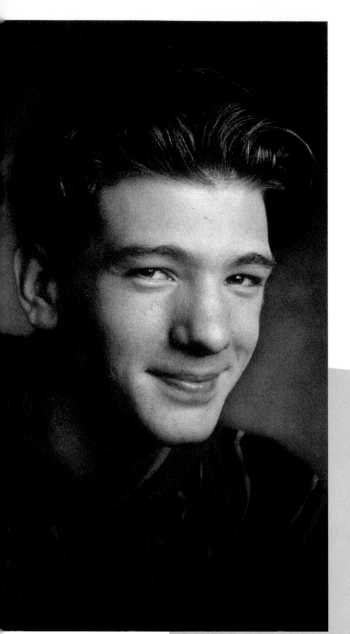

up and sing at an early age to his perfectionist tendencies. He was afraid he would give it his all and still not do a good job—not scared to get up in front of a crowd.

JC finally proved he was willing to hit the stage when a bunch of girls from his middle school asked him to dance with them in a talent competition. JC wasn't sure about it at first, but his friend Kacy dared him to do it and that was all the persuasion JC needed. The group won the competition and JC was hooked on performing.

More talent shows followed, and JC's group kept racking up the prizes and ribbons. Finally, JC agreed to enter the singing portion at one of the competitions. His parents were surprised, but proud that he was finally going to give it a try. He sang Richard Marx's "Right Here Waiting For You." "I won first place, twenty dollars from my friend Kacy, and had all these girls start calling me. I was like, 'Are you kidding? I'm going to keep doing this!'" JC told *Rolling Stone*.

Two weeks later, JC's mom told him she saw an ad for an open audition for *The Mickey Mouse Club*. Once

"... Somebody can be beautiful on the outside, but if they're not right on the inside, you don't need it."

—JC, in *Rolling Stone*

again, JC was dared by a friend to go for it and when his mom told him he could take the day off from school, he couldn't pass up the offer. "I really didn't expect to get the part," JC has said in *MMC Online*. "I only went to the audition because my friend wanted me to." At the casting call, JC was overwhelmed by the crowd of five hundred hopefuls. "I didn't think I had a chance because I had never done anything like it before," JC says in *'NSYNC: The Official Book*. "I got pretty lucky." At the end of a long day, one of the talent scouts took JC's mom aside and told her JC had a good shot at making the show. They asked twelve kids to stay and taped them singing a song, doing a quick dance number, and performing in a short skit. JC ended up being one of ten kids cast that year out of 20,000 that auditioned across the country.

JC and his dad moved to Orlando while his mom stayed in Maryland. JC says it was hard to be away from his mother and two younger siblings, but it also taught him to value family even more. Another big change that occurred as a result of *MMC* was the change of his name. JC had always been known to friends and family as Josh, but there was already a Josh on the show, so he came up with the name JC.

By all accounts, JC was a workaholic and a total goofball on the set. Behind the scenes he was best friends with Tony Lucca and Dale Godboldo and even thanks them in the liner notes of both 'NSYNC's albums. JC also became close with Keri Russell. "When I was on the Mouse Club, Keri Russell and I always did fun stuff together," JC told *Teen Online*.

Keri and JC rise above the crowd.

"It's incredible to meet performers who are just the nicest people in the world and are so down to earth."

—JC on the people he met on *MMC*, in *MMC Online*

JC was also friendly with fellow club member Jennifer McGill, who introduced him to Joey Fatone. And after JC completed two seasons on the Club, Justin was cast. JC often ponders what life would be like if he'd never gone to those *MMC* auditions in D.C. "You never know where your friendships might lead you," JC said in *MMC Online*.

But for this career-minded guy, the Club wasn't just about palling around. "It helped to prepare me for what I'm doing now," JC said in the same interview. "We filmed several shows every week, so I'm used to a heavy work schedule. Also, we produced an album and toured quite a bit, so I already know what life on the road is all about."

After the Club closed up for good, JC decided to focus on music, and went out to L.A. But it wasn't the best experience. "I got hooked up with some slimy people and got burned bad," JC told *Rolling Stone*. "Finally, I got in my car and left."

That's when he went to see Justin in Nashville and formed 'NSYNC. Now JC is dabbling in all areas of the music business. Not only did he do a lot of writing on "No Strings Attached," he also is producing songs with the all-girl group Wild Orchid. As for the future, JC has high hopes for 'NSYNC!

"If you're number one, there's nowhere to go but down. It's just a matter of, are you going to put the time in to climb back up?"

—JC, in *Teen People*

JC Facts

JC has been known to burst into spontaneous song in the middle of interviews.

All the members of 'NSYNC have the 'NSYNC flame tattooed on their ankles, except JC. He's petrified of needles.

"We all knew everyone there was talented, but we all could have gone back to our regular lives."—JC on life after *MMC*, in *Rolling Stone*

During 'NSYNC's first tour, JC went through a Buddy Holly phase, during which he constantly wore his jeans folded up and even bought himself a pair of black rectangular glasses.

JC loved to travel from an early age. Every summer his family would pile into the car and just go. As a result, JC has gotten to see the world's largest ball of twine, the largest rubber-band ball, and the largest bee farm.

JC was friends with fellow Mouseketeer Jason Minor when they were both growing up in the suburbs of Washington, D.C.

"I'm one of those freaks that believes that maybe one day when I meet 'the one' I'll know she's 'the one.'"—*Teen Online*

JC hasn't removed his good luck charm—a lion pendant—from his neck in over six years.

Christi

na Aguilera

Like Britney and Justin, Christina knew she was going to be a singer the moment she was old enough to know what singing was. Born in Staten Island, New York, Christina would lie on the floor of her bathroom and sing into a shampoo bottle. She'd line up her stuffed animals and use them as an audience. She sang to her parents, she sang to her neighbors, she sang to anyone who would listen.

Christina's mother plays the piano and the violin, so music was always in her blood, but she credits the film *The Sound of Music* for really inspiring her to sing. She first saw the film when she was five years old and absolutely loved it. At parties, little Christina would sing songs from

4th Grade; Rochester Elementary School, Rochester, PA

Full name: Christina Marie Aguilera

Birthday: December 18, 1980

Sign: Sagittarius

Birthplace: Staten Island, New York

Height: 5′

Hair: blond

Eyes: blue

Parents: mother, Shelly Kearns; father, Fausto Aguilera; stepfather, James Kearns

Siblings: sister, Rachel; stepsister, Stephanie; stepbrother, Casey; half-brother, Robert Michael

Favorite colors: pink, red, purple

Favorite foods: chili fries, burgers

Favorite music: R&B

Favorite performers: Mariah Carey, Whitney Houston, Limp Bizkit, Lauryn Hill, Brian McKnight

Favorite movies: *Mulan* (she performed a song for the soundtrack), *The Little Mermaid*

Favorite actors: Tom Hanks, Drew Barrymore

"[The idea of] 'Here today, gone tomorrow' sort of scares me. But I plan on working hard to make sure that doesn't happen."

—**Christina Aguilera, in *MTV Online***

the movie and everyone would applaud. From that time on, Christina knew she wanted to perform. She started singing at block parties and people would come up and ask her for her autograph, even though she wasn't yet old enough to sign her name!

The same year, Christina's family started moving around—a lot. Her dad was in the Army and he was transferred all over the place, from New Jersey to Texas to Japan. For three years, Christina basically lived out of a suitcase. When she was eight years old, her parents split up, and she, her mother, and her little sister Rachel moved to Rochester, Pennsylvania. That was where things really started to take off for her professionally.

First, Christina started making local appearances—more block parties and town events. Then, she attended an open casting call for—yep, you guessed

"I always wanted to work the window at a drive-thru fast food restaurant. I always thought it was a cool thing to do."

—Christina Aguilera, in *MTV Online*

it—*Star Search*. Christina nailed her audition and jetted off to Los Angeles to film the show where she performed Whitney Houston's "The Greatest Love of All." Unfortunately, it wasn't meant to be. "I lost . . . so that was a little devastating for an eight-year-old," Christina said in an *MTV Online* interview.

Fresh from her national TV performance, Christina was more psyched than ever to keep singing. But the kids at school weren't quite as thrilled for her. Christina was the subject of a lot of ridicule for her performing ways. She remembers being reduced to tears because of all the negative attention, but she loved performing so much, she kept working locally and tried to keep her chin up.

Then, in 1990, she attended an open audition for *The Mickey Mouse Club* in Pittsburgh. Like Britney, Christina was originally rejected because she was too young, but she never gave up on performing. At the age of eleven, she was the youngest person ever to sing the national anthem at a Pittsburgh Penguins game, and she did the same for the Steelers and the Pirates. And *MMC* never forgot about her. When she was twelve, Christina got a call saying that they still had a tape of her audition and asking whether she would like to audition again. Naturally, Christina jumped at the chance—and nailed it.

Christina loved her time on *The Mickey Mouse Club*. The first song she ever got to sing solo was "I Have Nothing"—a tune by her favorite artist of all time, Whitney Houston. And Christina couldn't wait to dance and act as well.

"The cast members were chosen to be in certain dance numbers, skits, songs, etc. in a number

The Three Mouseketeers with fellow *MMC* cast members.

" Aguilera has the makings of a true diva—someone who can back up the hype with some world-class pipes. The girl can just flat-out sing. "

—*MTV Online interview*

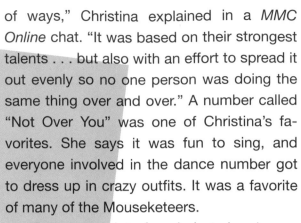

of ways," Christina explained in a *MMC Online* chat. "It was based on their strongest talents . . . but also with an effort to spread it out evenly so no one person was doing the same thing over and over." A number called "Not Over You" was one of Christina's favorites. She says it was fun to sing, and everyone involved in the dance number got to dress up in crazy outfits. It was a favorite of many of the Mouseketeers.

There was a lot of work, but she also remembers a ton of backstage pranks, joking around, ad-libbing on the set, and hanging with her new friends. Christina says there were on-and-off attractions behind the scenes, but almost everyone was too young to get very serious. There was also some bickering, but nothing big. "We all got along pretty well. Any fights we had were settled soon," Christina added in the same chat session. "We were just like brothers and sisters in that way."

"It was an overall great experience. I got to learn a lot more about the business, got national exposure, and it helped me mature in a lot of ways," Christina continued. "Also, I got to make some wonderful lifelong friends."

Among those friends was Britney Spears, whom Christina says she was (and is) very close with. She still talks to Britney and Nikki DeLoach of Innosense whenever she can. And her mother became tight with Tate Lynche's mom, so she spent a lot of time with him and still considers him to be a close friend. Today, Christina tries to catch 'NSYNC's and Britney's shows as often as possible, and is not at all surprised that so many of her fellow Mouseketeers hit it big. According to Christina, she and her friends

> **"I knew Britney and Christina would blow up. Britney was like a little Janet Jackson, and Christina was like a little Celine Dion."**
>
> —JC Chasez, in *Rolling Stone*

used to joke on the set about how one day they would all be huge stars.

Once the club closed its doors, Christina hit the road, performing in Japan and Europe. In 1997, Christina sang at the prestigious Golden Stag Festival in Brasov, Romania, representing the United States along with superstars Diana Ross and Sheryl Crow. Then, in 1998, in the same week she turned seventeen, Christina was hit with two bits of news that would change her life forever. First, she'd been chosen to sing the song "Reflection" for Disney's *Mulan* soundtrack—a song that would eventually be nominated for a Golden Globe Award and land Christina on all kinds of talk shows. Second, and even more heart-stopping, Christina signed her first record deal.

After recording "Reflection," Christina took off for L.A. and worked on her first album, *Christina Aguilera*, for six months. In the summer of 1999, her first single, "Genie in a Bottle," hung in at

> **"I had such great times with everybody both on and off camera. From rehearsals, to taping, to our free time and the things we did together, it was just one of the coolest times of my life!"**
>
> —Christina on *MMC*, in *MMC Online*

number one for five weeks, and her album flew to the number-one spot on the charts upon its release in August 1999. The album spawned four number-one hits, won Christina a Best New Artist Grammy and a Best New Artist Award at the American Latino Media Arts awards. Plus, it landed her on several MTV specials, got her a guest spot on *Beverly Hills 90210*, and fueled a wildly successful tour in the summer of 2000. Riding a huge wave of success, Christina released a Spanish-language album, *Mi Reflejo* in the fall of 2000, along with a Christmas album called *My Kind of Christmas*. She even taped her own Christmas special along with guest Brian McKnight, one of her favorite singers, which aired on ABC in December 2000.

At press time, Christina is hard at work on her fourth album, which she hopes to write and produce. There seems to be no stopping this tiny powerhouse.

Christina Facts

Christina is a huge sports fan, so performing at halftime at the Super Bowl in 2000 was like a dream come true.

When Christina heard that the *Mulan* producers were looking for a teen whose voice spanned more than two octaves, she made a tape of herself on a karaoke machine in her living room and her mom sent it off. She landed the job from that tape.

In 1999, Christina performed "The Christmas Song" for President Clinton on the TV special *Christmas at the White House*. Later, the president asked her to sing the first song on his millennium special, but Christina had to decline. She'd already made a commitment to be in Times Square and perform on MTV.

Christina's first album was one of the top ten best-selling albums of 1999, even though it was only out for five months.

Christina loves to play volleyball and tennis, and her favorite school subjects were science and English.

Christina was a Barbie fanatic growing up. Her favorite Christmas present ever was a Barbie kitchen.

Although Christina is twenty years old, she doesn't have her driver's license.

Keri

Russell

Keri Russell is not one of those former Mouseketeers who burst out of her crib performing. Born in Fountain Valley, California, Keri took dance lessons from an early age, but she didn't get serious about it until her parents moved her and her two siblings to Mesa, Arizona, when she was in junior high. According to Keri, dance was good for her self-esteem.

"I think it's hugely important for a teenage girl to have something more important in her life than junior high, which is a freak show for everyone," Keri told *In Style*. Dance was Keri's outlet. She took classes in everything—jazz, ballet, modern dance—and her natural talent began to shine through. While in Mesa, she joined a dance troupe called the Mesa Stars Dance and Drill Team. She practiced dance six to seven hours a day while still attending regular school, and traveled all over the country performing in halftime shows for the NBA and the NFL. The Stars also took Keri to Australia where she danced in Expo '88 at

Freshman year; Highlands Ranch High School, CO

> **"I see so many actors my age who are not enjoying their lives. I want to enjoy mine."**

— Keri Russell, in *In Style*

Full name: Keri Lynn Russell

Nickname: Care Bear (but only one friend ever called her that)

Birthday: March 23, 1976

Sign: Aries

Birthplace: Fountain Valley, California

Height: 5´4˝

Hair: light brown

Eyes: green

Parents: mother, Stephanie; father, David

Siblings: brother, Todd; sister, Julie

Favorite color: green

Favorite food: her family's barbecue

Favorite music: rock, folk

Favorite performers: Dave Matthews Band, U2, Sarah McLachlan

Favorite TV show: *ER*

Favorite movie: *High Fidelity*

Favorite actors: Susan Sarandon, Robert Duvall

the World's Fair. It was a crazy time for Keri, who was just twelve years old, but her experience with the Stars solidified her love of dance and performing.

Just before Keri started high school, her family picked up and moved again, this time to Denver, Colorado. She says that her high school experience helps her relate to her character on *Felicity*. By her own account, Keri was kind of a loner with one best friend. It was the perfect time to throw herself full force into dance. She won numerous scholarships and found herself taking up to seventeen classes per week at prestigious dance studios in Denver. From that point on, dancing was a huge part of her identity.

When she was fourteen, a photographer saw Keri dance and asked if she'd like to get into modeling. Never one to turn down a new experience, Keri gave it a shot—and hated it. Still, modeling led to an appearance on *Star Search*, and soon Keri knew she wanted to be a performer. She auditioned for *The Mickey Mouse Club* at the age of fifteen, and impressed the talent scouts so much, she landed a position as a Mouseketeer, and was soon offered a part in her first feature film, *Honey, I Blew Up the Kid*.

Heading to Orlando was a no-brainer for Keri, a girl who thrives on new challenges. And being so close to Disney World was an added perk. "It was pretty exciting for a sixteen-year-old," Keri said in a *TV Guide* interview. "Plus, we got to go on rides for free." In her three seasons, Keri was a featured dancer in countless production numbers, but she never sang lead in any songs. "We all had our strengths and dance was definitely my strength," Keri said in an AOL online chat session. "People like Christina, JC, and Justin . . . they were the singers."

Even if she never belted out a tune, Keri did have other responsibilities on the show beyond dancing. While on the Club, Keri discovered another love—acting. Keri learned a lot from the acting coach on the set, Gary Spatz, and enjoyed testing her acting chops in

"I don't have to go somewhere to have fun as long as I'm with friends."

—Keri Russell, in *MMC Online*

Emerald Cove and in the comedic skits. By the time she left the Club, Keri knew she wanted to become an actor.

But a new goal wasn't the only thing Keri took away from her years on the *MMC*. Her favorite thing about being on the Club was hanging out with her friends. "JC was one of my best friends," Keri said on AOL. "When I was sixteen years old, I'd just gotten my car and we'd drive around everywhere together." Keri and JC still keep in touch, and Keri also counts fellow Mouseketeer Ilana Miller as one of her closest confidantes.

Then, of course, there was Tony Lucca. "It was always Keri and Tony," Ilana told *In Style* in 1999. "They come as a package."

Keri and Tony were often paired up as boyfriend and girlfriend in skits and music videos on the Club, and had an on-again, off-again relationship for years. They even lived together in L.A. before they finally split up in 2000.

When Keri left the Club in 1993, she moved to Los Angeles by herself to see if she could make it as an actor. She soon landed a role as one of Dudley Moore's three daughters in the short-lived sitcom *Daddy's Girls* and taped a live-action pilot based on Kevin Smith's indie film *Clerks*. After that, there were guest stints on shows like *Boy Meets World*, *Married . . . With Children*, and *7th Heaven*.

In 1996, Keri was cast in Aaron Spelling's series *Malibu Shores* along with Tony Lucca who had moved to L.A. after *MMC* wrapped. At the time, *Beverly Hills*

JC and Keri hanging out with the gang.

90210 and *Melrose Place* were huge hits and everyone thought *Malibu Shores* was going to be Spelling's next smash. Unfortunately, it only lasted eight episodes and Keri landed back on the audition circuit.

Luckily, Keri always seemed to find work. She appeared in a string of TV movies and had a starring role in the independent flick *Eight Days a Week*. In 1997, Keri appeared in a FOX series called *Roar*, which had a minor cult following, but Keri's role didn't bode well for her future television career—she was killed off in the first episode. After that, Keri appeared in another independent movie called *The Curve*.

Well before *Felicity* debuted on the WB, Keri's face was everywhere. There were commercials, billboards, and magazine covers. The show hadn't even hit the air and people were coming up to Keri and asking for her autograph—what if *Felicity* wasn't the hit everyone predicted it would be?

"Seriously, I was really worried about that," Keri told *TV Guide*. "If the show went bad, I would *really* look bad because I'm the main character. If it bombed, people would say, 'That Keri Russell series was really *bad*.' Who needs that kind of pressure? But I think I made the right choice."

No arguments there. Not only does Keri have a great time playing TV's favorite college student, she also won a Golden Globe for her work on the first season of the show.

As for the future, Keri just wants to keep learning and doing whatever makes her happy. She still loves to dance when she can find the time, but says she's glad it's not part of her job. Right now, Keri is reading movie scripts and auditioning for various roles.

"I want to find the next film project that challenges me and is still acceptable to my idealism," Keri told *In Style*. "I really hope I find it."

With talent like Keri's, finding that role shouldn't be a problem.

"She was the first one to fray her jeans, which was really cool at the time. And she was so beautiful, we were just in awe of her."

—Christina Aguilera, in *YM*

Keri Facts

Keri has an easy, comfortable style and is usually found in jeans and Birkenstocks without a bit of makeup.

Keri loves her alone time, whether she's reading, walking, or going to see movies by herself on Sunday afternoons.

According to Keri, the best thing about acting is getting to meet new and interesting people. The worst thing? Kissing people she doesn't think are funny or cute or that she has no connection with.

Keri and Tony played a couple on *Malibu Shores,* but they were actually broken up at the time and barely even speaking.

In a 1997 online interview, Keri said that if she could be someone else for a day she'd be someone "crazy" like Lenny Kravitz. —*Universal chat*

Keri's favorite moments on *Felicity* are when the whole group is together and it gets crazy and funny and emotional. She also likes the "cheesy romantic stuff."—*AOL online chat*

Keri is named after her grandfather, Kermit.

Keri almost didn't get the part on *Felicity* because she was too pretty. "The character was always intended to be played by someone who was plain-looking. Keri is so gorgeous. She was too attractive to play Felicity, yet she couldn't have been more right. She is so natural, funny, and engaging."—J.J. Abrams, Executive Producer, in *people.com*'s "50 Most Beautiful People"

Where Are They Now?

The fab five featured in this book aren't the only Mouseketeers making names for themselves on the entertainment scene. Here's a rundown of what some of the others have been doing since their days in Orlando.

Albert (Fields): Albert was one of five members of the pop group The Party, who recorded their last album in 1993. He released a solo album under the name Jeune in 1995.

Blain (Carson): Blain is now known as Jason Carson and released his first independent album, *So Sick of This* in 1999. He is now working on a follow-up and also had a costarring role in the independent film *The End*. Check out his Web site at www.jasoncarson.com

Brandy (Brown): After leaving the Club, Brandy played the role of Angela Corelli on the now defunct soap opera *Another World*. She graduated from the University of Alabama and currently lives in Louisiana with her husband.

Chase (Hampton): Chase was also a member of the group The Party and has guest-starred on various television shows, including *Buffy the Vampire Slayer* and *The X Files*. He now sings lead for the group Buzzfly, which has released two independent albums. Check out the Buzzfly Web site at www.buzzfly.com

Dale (Godboldo): Dale was one of the stars of *Jenny*, the short-lived Jenny McCarthy sitcom, and the UPN sitcom, *Shasta McNasty*

He's also appeared in feature films including *Cold Hearts* and *The Young Unknowns* and made a cameo appearance in 'NSYNC's video *I Drive Myself Crazy*.

Damon (Pampolina): Damon appeared on MTV's *Undressed* in July 2000.

David (Kater): David appeared in *Sister Act 2* with Lauryn Hill and Jennifer Love Hewitt. He is now a member of the recording group *Unity*, who contributed a single to the soundtrack for the MTV movie *2Gether*.

Deedee (Magno): Deedee was a member of The Party and has appeared in feature films and on television, including a guest spot on *Third Watch*. She played the lead part of Kim in *Miss Saigon* on Broadway until July 2000 and is currently working on putting together a solo album and exploring other theater projects.

Fred (Newman): Fred provides the voices for Skeeter and Mr. Dink, among others, on the popular cartoon *Doug*. He can also be seen on the PBS network's children's program *Between the Lions*.

Ilana (Miller): Ilana attends New York University as a general studies student. She made a brief appearance in the Miramax film *54*.

Jason (Minor): Jason is a member of a four-part harmony group called Southbound, which is based in Nashville.

Jennifer (McGill): Jennifer graduated from New York University and is now working on an album.

Kevin (Osgood): Kevin graduated from the University of Southern California School of Cinema-Television in June 1997. He now has his own production company specializing in Christian music videos.

Marc (Worden): Marc had a role in TNT's film *The Pirates of Silicon Valley*, provides voices for the animated show *Batman Beyond*, and made guest appearances on *Felicity* and *Star Trek: Deep Space Nine*.

Matt (Morris): Matt is touring with his father, country singer Gary Morris. Together they are releasing a Christmas album and Matt is working on a Spanish-language solo album.

Mowava (Pryor): Mowava has appeared in numerous commercials and has made TV guest appearances, including one on *Touched by an Angel*.

Mylin (Brooks): Mylin made a brief appearance in the film *Starship Troopers* and has two albums out in Japan.

Nikki (DeLoach): Nikki is a member of the group Innosense, who released their first album, *So Together*, in 2000. The group also opened for 'NSYNC at various stops on their *No Strings Attached* tour.

Nita (Booth): Nita was named first runner-up in the 1998 Miss Virginia pageant. She eventually succeeded to the title when Miss Virginia won the Miss America pageant.

Rhona (Bennett): Rhona has a recurring role on *The Jamie Foxx Show* on the WB. She has also signed a recording deal with Darkchild Entertainment.

Ricky (Luna): Ricky appeared in the movie of the week *The Elián González Story* and has made guest appearances on *Angel* and *Judging Amy*. He is also a member of a vocal trio based in Los Angeles.

Ryan (Gosling): Ryan starred as Hercules in the syndicated TV show *Young Hercules*. He also appeared as Alan Bosley in Denzel Washington's hit film, *Remember the Titans*, and is featured in *The Believer*, a film due out in 2001.

Tate (Lynche): Tate was a dancer in the Las Vegas production of *Notre-Dame de Paris* and now appears in *Disney's The Lion King* on Broadway.

Terra (McNair): In 1998, Terra released a solo album titled *Pulled Apart* under the name Terra Deva.

Tony (Lucca): Tony is a songwriter and recording artist and has recently signed a deal with Knatomic Records.

SOURCES:

San Jose Mercury News, April 18, 1989; *TV Guide*, April 21, 1990; *Teen Beat; Britney Spears Stylin'* (Warner Books, 1999); *ELLE*, October 2000; *POP People: Britney!* (Scholastic, 2000); *Britney Spears' Heart to Heart* (Three Rivers Press, 2000); *PEOPLEONLINE/Britney*, February 15, 1999; *COSMOGIRL*, November 2000; *'NSYNC: The Official Book* (BDDFYR, 1998); *People.com/'NSync*, February 8, 1999; *COSMOGIRL online; MMC online; Rolling Stone '98; Teen Magazine Online*, March 2000; *Teen People*, Summer 2000; *Rolling Stone*, March 20, 2000; *Christina-a.com; YM*, August 1999; *MTV Online/Christina Aguilera* interview, Spring 1999 and Fall 1999; *In Style*, August 1999; *In Style*, Summer 2000 (makeover issue); *JANE*, October 1999; *Entertainment Weekly*, 1998 Year-End Special; *PEOPLE.com/*"50 Most Beautiful People," 1999; *TV Guide*, November 7, 1998; *Universal Chat*, June 24, 1997